the Secret Code

written by
Dana Meachen Rau

illustrated by
Bari Weissman

SCHOLASTIC INC.
New York   Toronto   London   Auckland   Sydney
Mexico City   New Delhi   Hong Kong   Buenos Aires

For Derek, who sees more than I ever will —D. M. R.

To my beloved Ida, the sweetest dog ever —B. W.

Reading Consultant
Linda Cornwell
Learning Resource Consultant, Indiana Department of Education

AUTHOR'S NOTE:

Blind people are not able to read books the same way many people do, because they cannot see with their eyes. So in 1829, Louis Braille, a blind French student, published a simple code based on a system of six raised dots (⠿). He made it possible for blind people to read by touch.

On pages 22 and 23, you can see that the letters of the Braille alphabet are different combinations of these six dots. Check your local library for a Braille book that you can feel on your own!

ISBN 0-516-24141-9

12 11 10 9 8 7 6 5 4 3 2 1   2 3 4 5 6 7/0

Printed in the U.S.A.   10

First Scholastic club printing, May 2002

Oscar can read a secret code.

Lucy saw it when Oscar
opened his book.

4

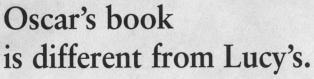

Oscar's book
is different from Lucy's.

Lucy's page has black letters.
She reads with her eyes.

The girl and her dog ran and ran and ran as fast as they could go.

Oscar's page is covered with bumps.
He reads with his fingers!

12

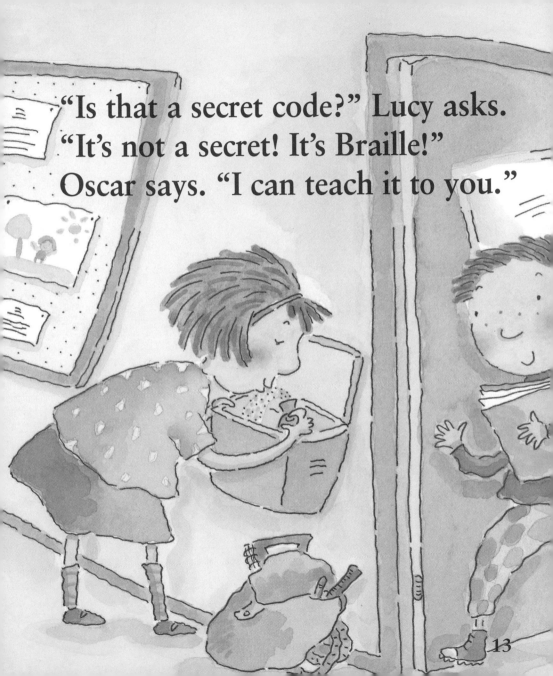

"Is that a secret code?" Lucy asks.
"It's not a secret! It's Braille!"
Oscar says. "I can teach it to you."

13

14

Each set of bumps is a letter.
Together, they form words.

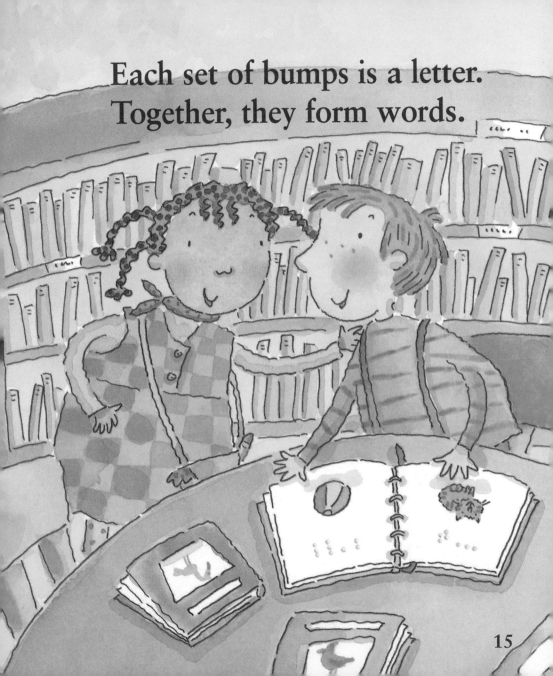

"Just like my letters!" Lucy says.

Oscar is blind,
so he doesn't see the letters.
He feels them.

When Lucy learns a b c,
Oscar learns ° ᣬ °°.

21

a b c d e

f g h i j

k l m n o

p q r s t

u v w x y

z capital period
   sign

23

Now Lucy knows the secret code.

25

Oscar can write notes to Lucy . . .

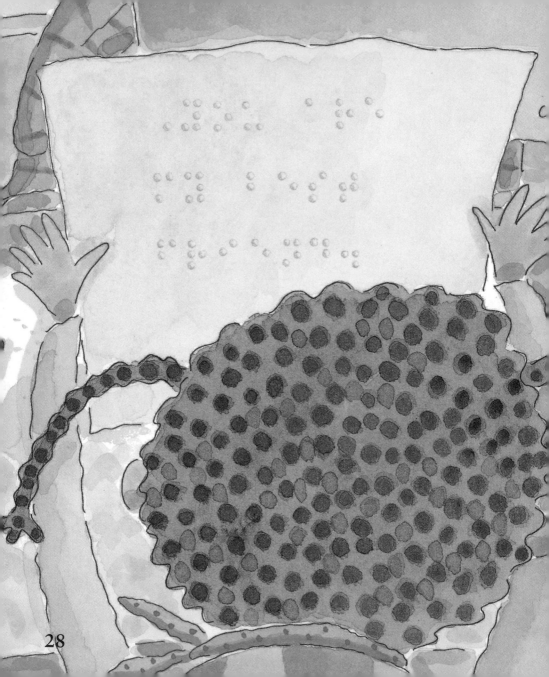

. . . and Lucy can read the message.

31

WORD LIST (66 WORDS)

	each	it	now	she
a	eyes	it's	of	so
and	feels	just	opened	teach
asks	fingers	knows	Oscar	that
black	form	learns	Oscar's	the
blind	from	letter	page	them
book	fun	letters	read	they
Braille	has	like	reading	to
bumps	he	Lucy	read	together
can	her	Lucy's	saw	when
code	his	message	says	with
covered	I	my	secret	words
different	is	not	see	write
doesn't	isn't	notes	set	you

ABOUT THE AUTHOR

Dana Meachen Rau is the author of many books for children. She also works as a children's book editor and lives with her husband, Chris, in Southbury, Connecticut. Dana's brother, Derek, is blind. When they were kids, Derek taught Dana how to read Braille. (She reads it with her eyes, not her fingers!) Dana has always been impressed by, and often boasts about, her brother's ability to read in the dark!

ABOUT THE ILLUSTRATOR

Bari Weissman has illustrated approximately twenty children's books in her twenty-year career. To research Braille for this book, she visited Perkins School for the Blind in Massachusetts and looked at the Braille books there. Bari lives in Boston Massachusetts, with her husband, Warren, and their cat, Ishkabbible.